HAPPY BIRTHDAY, DOUGAL

HarperCollins *Children's Books*

First published in Great Britain in 2005 by HarperCollins Children's Books.
HarperCollins Children's Books is a division of HarperCollins Publishers Ltd.
Creative Consultant Liz Keynes
1 3 5 7 9 10 8 6 4 2

0-00-718356-9
A CIP catalogue for this title is available from the British Library.
Printed and bound in China

It was a beautiful sunny day in the Enchanted Village and everyone was very happy.

Everyone, that is, except Dougal the little dog. He was NOT very happy at all.

It was his birthday. His best friend Florence had told him all about birthdays.

"Birthdays are special," she had said, "and everyone who loves you gives you lovely cards and wonderful presents."

But the trouble was, no one seemed to know it was HIS birthday TODAY.

No one had given him wonderful presents, and no one had sent him a lovely card.

Just then, he saw Ermintrude the cow.
Maybe she had remembered?

Y-BONBON

"Beeeoootiful day," trilled Ermintrude.

"It is a beautiful day," said Dougal, "my special day, in fact..."

"Why's that?" asked Ermintrude with a secretive smile. "Are you coming to my show?"

With that, she started singing. Very badly.

Dougal sighed and slunk off.

Then he almost tripped over Dylan.

"Hey!" groaned Dylan sleepily, "take it easy man!"

"Easy!" said Dougal, "but it's my..." But Dylan had closed his eyes again.

"Huh!" said Dougal. "When is that rabbit ever awake?"

"Florence!" beamed Dougal, spotting his friend across the street. "She must have remembered my birthday!"

"Hello Dougal!" called Florence, smiling at the downhearted dog. "Can't stop, lots to do!" And she skipped off.

"Galloping sugar lumps! What about my birthday?" shouted Dougal.

Now Dougal was really miserable.
No one cared that it was his birthday.
Not even Florence.

Suddenly he remembered something.
The candy-seller would be coming on his tricycle to deliver the sweets to the village today!

What had Florence said about birthdays?

Florence said you got presents on your birthday.

If no one wanted to give him a present, then he'd get one for himself.

He knew just what he wanted most in the whole world.

But he hadn't much time...

Dougal looked
to the right.

Then he looked
to the left.

Then he took a pin
out of one of Ermintrude's
concert posters and hurried out
of the Town Square.

DIVA
CONCERT

Then he heard it! There was the hum of an engine in the distance. Dougal ran faster. The hum was now a growl.

BRRRRRRRRRRRRRRRRR

The candy-seller and his tricycle, loaded with goodies, were roaring towards him.

RRRRRRRRRRRRRRRRRR

Dougal raced into the middle of the road, and dropped the pin, spike side up. He flopped down behind a tree, out of breath.

The tricycle whizzed past, nearly squashing his nose.

Then there was a huge...

BANG... CRASH!

The tricycle crashed and there were sweeties everywhere!

"Oh, dear. I'd better go and get help," said the candy-seller.

"And I'll – er – stay here and look after all the sweets," mumbled Dougal.

He couldn't believe it. This was the best birthday present ever.

"DOUGAL!"

Guiltily, Dougal looked around as Florence came running down the road.

"Nothing wrong, nothing to see!" he called out.

He tried to sit on the sweets but there were too many to hide.

Florence looked at the sweets in the road and gasped.

"Oh, no, whatever happened?" she cried. "These are supposed to be your birthday present from all of us! An extra special delivery of your favourite yummy sweets!"

Dougal

Dougal stared at the sea of sweets. They were all meant for him!

"The candy-seller was supposed to deliver them to your surprise party on The Magic Roundabout!" said Florence. "I've been looking for you everywhere!"

Dougal sighed happily. "So you hadn't forgotten after all!"

“Of course not,” said Florence, giving Dougal a great, big hug. “Happy birthday, Dougal! Now help me pick up all these sweets!”

THE MAGIC ROUNDABOUT™
Coming soon to all good toy & gift shops
There's more to this rabbit than meets the eye!
Light Activated Room Guard DYLAN™
Gift Boxed Mugs
Character Beanies
Bouncing ZEBEDEE™
Zebedee still has some spring in his step!
Press my tummy to hear me talk!
Talking FLORENCE™
ERMINTRUDE™ Back Pack
Lots of fun sounds and silly phrases!
Talk'n Sing ERMINTRUDE™
See Dougal™ spin on the spot!
Remote Control DOUGAL™
ViViD imaginations
Colour and specification may change.